"Action-packed and full of thrill."
David H.

"An easy recommendation for anything that knows how to read."
Ahmad G.

"Unique concept with tonnes of potential to be a great series. Fast paced and full of action!"
Marcus H.

"Brilliantly written book and a wonderful snack for the imagination."
Ianis V.

"Had me wishing I was special too. Five stars."
Mattias H.

Copyright © 2023 Jonathan Harii

All rights reserved.

Cover design by Ahmad Ghaddar

No part of this book can be reproduced in any form or by written, electronic or mechanical, including photocopying, recording, or by any information retrieval system without written permission in writing by the author.

Although every precaution has been taken in the preparation of this book, the publisher and author assume no responsibility for errors or omissions. Neither is any liability assumed for damages resulting from the use of information contained herein.

ISBN 979-8-8594-9555-9

AGAINST THE ODDS

JONATHAN HARII

—Emma

For all the Kool Kids

Consider this to be a prequel to the actual books that may or may not be published one day.

All proceeds go to the

Mark Evison Foundation

CONTENTS

1	Busted	5
2	9 Ash Lane	9
3	Powers…?	18
4	Experimentation	35
5	Casino Heist	53
6	Sore losers	80

BUSTED

"Daniel!"

The cry invaded Daniel's focus, as he sat sprawled at his computer furiously clicking his mouse. On the screen in front of him, Daniel's character was shooting other players as he navigated a thick jungle, the carnage and movement stopping abruptly as, sighing, Daniel took off his headphones and stood up.

As he procrastinated answering his mother's call, he looked around his room, typically messy for a 17-year-old, walls ordained by various achievements and revision notes, shuddering at what could have caused his mother to think of him.

By the time Daniel trudged onto the landing, down the stairs, and into the living room, his mother had grown a furious red at the face, with eyes bulging and spittle flying, "How dare you keep me waiting, have you seen your school report?!", Daniel groaned inwardly – he knew that he had failed his exams but had done everything to keep his mother from knowing. He had collected mail from the mailbox every day before she could get to it, intercepted phone calls from the school and forged his own progress reports, delaying the inevitable. "You have seriously breached my trust, all those hours spent 'revising', fruitless!", His mother was becoming increasingly hysterical with every glance at his red-marked report sheet, "From now on, you will refocus time on studying and school – absolutely no more gaming until things change." Daniel stood inanimately absorbing the barrage of words, he should have known that the chances of his mother remaining passive to the lack of communication from the school about his report were slim to none, especially since two weeks have gone by since the deadline to receive school reports-

"Daniel, are you listening to me? Your every waking hour will be spent revising until I see a – hey where are you

goin-!"

Her monologue was interrupted by the harsh retort of the front door slamming shut. Daniel had left, leaving his mother like a sailboat breaking free from the relentless grip of a tempest.

It was unusually cold outside, flying in the face of the weather forecast projected by several news outlets. Daniel reflected on the punishment given by his mother, a ban from his computer? He felt like he and his mother had drifted apart since his exams, he was always studious and had the highest grades in his year group before his apparent downfall. The breeze buffeted him, summoning goosebumps onto Daniel's exposed arms, as he retrieved his phone from his pocket and punched the screen once, twice, calling. While waiting for the line to pick up, Daniel thought about the events leading up to this moment and how some bad luck meant that bullies had hijacked his life lately, including forcing him to miss all his exams, giving him an immediate fail. Of course, he hadn't been able to explain this to anybody else except his friend, Jesse, and only after he swore not to tell anybody else.

"Hey Jesse...usual spot?... see you in five."

Walking over the cracked and tired sidewalk, Daniel slipped his phone back into his pocket as he turned the corner onto Ash Lane, as stated by a faded, tilted sign gate-guarding the mouth of the road. He increased his pace, making sure to avoid eye contact with the various drunken figures that littered the pavement, faces deformed by the alcohol and drug abuse that was all too rampant in this area. The trees lining the road were wrinkled with age, standing hunched over the street, quietly invading the surface beneath them with a steady cascade of leaves, whose verdant green contrasted with the monochrome appearance of the black road, grey pavement and the grey faces of those of trapped by addiction.

Crack.

Without looking down, Daniel knew he had stepped on another empty syringe that lay scattered haphazardly over the path. It was already dark outside, but Daniel was not afraid of the dangers of late-night walking, he knew this area better than he felt he knew himself.

9 ASH LANE

Reaching the end of Ash Lane, Daniel approached a severely dilapidated home that was clearly abandoned; there was not a single window that was not broken, and its walls were shamelessly ordained by graffiti tags, bar the occasional Instagram engraving and confession of love. This was it. Daniel's second home.

Without hesitation, Daniel leaped over the chained gate, dodged the overgrown stinging nettles and pulled open the rotting wooden door, verifying his location with a glance to the door number, a slightly offset 9 consumed by corrosion and red rust, camouflaging with the dirty red, peeling paint of the front door. A loud squeal announced the new visitor to the darkness that lay within, prompting a series of screeches and groans, signature to the flexing of ancient floorboards underneath footsteps, that began making their way towards the entrance. Daniel stepped over the threshold into the home, embracing the rotting, putrid smell of the interior, people rarely came here, but when they did, they left their mark. He allowed the door to swing shut behind him and began moving towards the sound of what had to be Jesse's footsteps, "Jesse, man, I don't know what to do." Creak. "My mum's found out about my grades and she's -" As Daniel talked, he continued walking deeper into the house, the stale air settling into his clothes, navigating with his phone's flashlight through the maze of corridors to meet the approaching footsteps. He had briefly wondered why his friend had not said anything, but before he could act upon his suspicions, he froze, motionless, mouth forming a perfect 'o' as emerging from the darkness, was not his friend's flashlight and his shorter-than-average stature, but rather a silhouette well over 6 feet tall, towering over him.

The darkness seemed to palpitate with life, pushing against Daniel's phone flashlight as he continued to stare in terror at the massive form in front of him. Where was Jesse? The shadow continued moving forwards, marked by the protests from the floorboards beneath it, stretching out an abnormally long arm until it stopped, leaving a slender finger inches away from Daniel's nose. Even this close to Daniel, not a single feature remained uncovered by the bottomless, inky black that enveloped the figure. However, the substance of the silhouette had become easier to distinguish, its body consisted of a black smoke like that of a thundercloud or from an oil refinery. Tendrils of the inky smoke expelled from the finger and began drifting towards Daniel's nostrils, invertedly reeled in by his panicked breathing. His heart pounded in his chest, as if trying to break from Daniel's ribcage and do what he was failing to do – flee. Each breath he took drew the swirling darkness deeper into his lungs, leaving him unable to breathe. Daniel wanted to scream for help but only a strangled gargle escaped his lips, he twitched in protest as his body refused to obey, seemingly paralysed in fear.

Suddenly, a faint sound echoed through the house, a distant but distinct voice calling Daniel's name. Jesse. Daniel blinked and finally found his voice, managing to scream out, "Jesse! Help me!". The cry pierced the suffocating silence, and the thing recoiled as if startled, withdrawing its wisps of smoke, back into its humanoid mass. The darkness that pulsated around Daniel's torch was no longer as invasive, losing its light-choking blackness with every one of Jesse's hurried footsteps towards Daniel.

However, the silhouette, seemingly realising its illusion of fear had been shattered, had begun to expand, abandoning the crude resemblance to a human figure. Its mass drew in the rouge wisps of smoke rising from its body, and then like a bullet from the barrel of a smoking gun, rushed towards Daniel with extraordinary speed. Daniel rose his arms to protect his face, however it was futile, the smoke heaved around his block and forced itself back into Daniel's nose. His lungs went cold as the smog pushed itself down his throat, immune to his attempts to snort it back out, trumping the oxygen that Daniel's body desperately needed – he was being suffocated. Sparks began to fly over Daniel's vision and his hearing became tinny and cheap as he stood clawing at the invading smoke in vain. The footfall become louder and the smoke's intensity with which it pushed itself into

Daniel's lungs grew, forcing every last wisp to enter Daniel's body before the new arrival.

As Jesse entered the room, Daniel was on the floor coughing and spluttering, gesturing towards his neck. Jesse had never listened in class, especially when they had taught lifesaving techniques. Instead relying on his YouTube viewership, he positioned himself behind Daniel, drew his arm back, and slapped him with full force on his back. Daniel swore. "Stop! Stop! STOP!" Jesse froze with his arm poised above Daniel, ready to deliver another blow. Daniel groaned and rolled over. He felt strange. His body fizzed with exhilarating energy. Arms shaking with the desperation of a chain smoker struggling to open a cigarette packet, he stood up. "What happened?", Jesse asked, breaking the uncomfortable silence, Daniel's veins were no longer their natural colour, but rather they had become black, with the veins themselves protruding from his face. His eyes had a nervous twitch, and his hands were violently shaking. "What were you choking on?", Jesse pressed. "Nothing."

"Should I call an ambulance?", without waiting for a response, Jesse had already dialled 999 and was ready to call when Daniel shook his head,

"No, I'm fine, I'm going home." Daniel's voice trembled as he spoke, his words punctuated by short breaths.

"But-"

He raised his arm, stopping Jesse from talking. "I'm going home, alone, I'll - text you later." Hesitantly, Jesse nodded, eyes wide with concern as they watched Daniel shuffle towards the front door and leave. Jesse scrambled after him as the house was filled with a deafening silence, but Daniel was already out of reach, disappearing into the night. Jesse vaulted over the front gate and stood, framed by the overgrown mess of nettles behind him, torn between chasing after his friend and respecting his wish for solitude.

Daniel arrived at his front door in what seemed like seconds. He felt lightheaded almost as if the smoke had not only penetrated his lungs but also his brain. Daniel paused, confused, surely he should be dead after inhaling so much smoke? Some part of his brain refused to compute his encounter– Daniel, a voice called. Daniel froze. He tentatively looked around – not a single soul. He was going crazy. He fumbled in his pockets for his key, wrestled it into the lock and pushed his front door open revealing his mother. The ceiling lights emitted a cold, harsh light, beaming down upon Daniel, scrutinising, condemning. She stood at the foot of the stairs, bearing a surprisingly anxious face, staring daggers at Daniel's miserable figure.

As Daniel tentatively nudged the door closed, the paintings that lined the entrance hallway seemed to frown in disapproval, even the flowers by the front door appeared to be wilting in protest to Daniel's dramatic earlier exit. However, his mother's eyes softened when she saw his bedraggled state. "Daniel, what's wrong?" His mother spoke slowly as if Daniel was some wild animal, unpredictable and closed to reason. Daniel looked down, avoiding his mother's gaze "Nothing." He furtively brought his sodden arms, blemished by blackened veins, behind his back preventing any awkward questions and disguising it as an attempt to appear guilty. His mother shifted her position, crossing her arms over her chest – restraining her motherly instinct. Daniel tensed.

"You left me while I was speaking, you didn't tell me where you went, and you come back at this time?".

Time? Confused Daniel, turned 180 degrees, looking above the front door where the clock hung. Twelve twenty. Daniel's heart thudded. He had stormed out at about seven o'clock, he vaguely remembered, glancing at his watch. How had 5 hours passed? He swivelled back around. "You've proven to me that you no longer respect me" his mother hammered on, as if Daniel was a misshapen lump of steel that needed to be corrected. "You are grounded to your room until further notice." This blow barely dented Daniel's outlook, he spent most of his time in his room anyways - "And the Wi-Fi router...", Daniel breathed in, "...will stay downstairs, off, until something changes." The final blow made sparks; Daniel was chronically online. "Now go to your room, we'll talk more in the morning". His mother had just condemned him to solitary confinement. Sending him to his holding cell like a Judge sentencing a criminal. However, Daniel didn't protest. Sill aware of his abnormal appearance, he continued to avert his gaze, hide his bare arms and rushed past his mother upstairs to his room.

POWERS...?

Making sure to slam his bedroom door behind him, Daniel flipped on his light switch and plonked himself onto his bed, fishing his phone out of his pocket. Five missed calls from Jesse, spanning from eight to eleven pm. Daniel shook his head, wondering what had happened to him in the house, it seemed that not only did it affect him physically with blackened veins which were probably not a good sign at all, but also mentally. Without thinking, Daniel called Jesse. "Hello?"

An audible groan was heard from the other line "Do you know what time it is?", Jesse angrily whispered, "I've been trying to get hold of you all evening and you wouldn't pick up."

"Yeah… sorry – just wanted to let you know that I'm fine, don't worry about me."

"Ok." There was a pause, "Guess I'll speak to you tomorrow then, goodnight." Before Daniel could answer, the line was cut off. He placed his phone on his bed and stared at the ceiling, its perfect white framed by the disarray of his room, visible even on the tops of his cabinets and shelves. Daniel thought of how he would explain his encounter with the entity to Jesse, sighing, he realised that he would sound insane. After all, here they were in the modern world, where scientific discoveries were rife and the fictionalisation of the supernatural was pursued relentlessly, and yet, Daniel doubted what he had experienced was anything less than unexplainable.

Suddenly, his brain exploded in pain, screeching against his skull in agony- Daniel. The voice boomed, rattling his teeth. Daniel desperately bit his lip restraining the cry of pain that wanted to escape his throat. Flip a coin. Daniel scrambled off his bed and onto his bedroom floor, cushioned by the carpet of discarded clothing, franticly pulling out drawers and pockets for a coin. Lifting a forgotten diary from the bottom of his bedside drawer, Daniel finally found what he was looking for. An old, grubby two pence. "Daniel, are you alright?" His mother called, punctuated by a series of knocks on his door, he had woken his mother up with his movement. "I- uh – fell out of my bed" Daniel lied instinctively, thanking himself for the mess on the floor of his room which blocked light from escaping through the gap at the bottom of his door, giving credibility to his story and saving him from experiencing additional wrath from his mother. "Do you need anything?" His mother pursued, surprising Daniel with her alternating attitude. One moment she was an iron lady the other she was unwavering in her desire to nurture. "No, mum, goodnight" Daniel replied, partly trying to get rid of her and partly still stinging from his punishment.

Daniel stayed in his position, clutching the coin, until his mother's footsteps receded. It had the ordinary brass texture and appearance of any old coin, bearing the expected bite marks and scratches. The smell of the coin was iconic, whispering of hundreds of miles travelled and boasting a palimpsest of countless fingerprints. Daniel closed his eyes, probing within himself, searching for the voice. Nothing. "Guess I flip it then" The coin arced through the air, a perfect launch, its copper finish glinting in the bedroom light as time seemed to slow. Instinctively, Daniel guessed the outcome, tails, as he watched the coin's descent back down onto his open palm. Tails. Daniel blinked in mild surprise at his correct guess, but quickly furrowed his brow. Why did he have to flip a coin? Your gamble is correct, your luck has increased. The voice boomed and suddenly, like a weight being lifted off a trampoline, the tension that had persisted in the back of Daniel's skull evaporated.

Daniel sat there, clutching the coin between his middle and forefinger, bewildered. He glanced at the coin. Guess the outcome, the more likely the outcome you want will occur, the voice whispered, no longer booming thunder, but instead a gentle nudge. "What are you?" The voice paused, a low humming filling the silence, before it replied, A god. I have chosen you to bear some of my power, it's up to you to use it. This is hopefully the last you will hear from me, have fun. Have fun? Daniel's mind spun. For a god, the voice seemed oddly informal, and keen to move on from his background. For a god he expected the heavens to open and release a celestial light, doves to fly and perhaps a choir of angels but this 'god' had nothing, giving him a dubious power and a severe migraine.

Unless there was no god that visited him and Daniel was instead going mad and hallucinating. He pushed himself up from his sitting position, joints protesting at the sudden movement, and glanced at his bed, eyes landing on his alarm clock. Three am. It was sleeping deprivation paired with smoke inhalation, then. How had he lost track of time so badly? It seemed only minutes since Daniel had slammed his door and pretended to go to sleep. Determined to get some rest, Daniel turned off his alarm clock and flopped onto his bed, teeth unbrushed and wearing clothes caked in events of the day. Immediately falling asleep.

His dormancy was empty, no dreams to entertain him, to fill in the gap between the closing and opening of eyes. Three loud knocks awoke him. Daniel sat up, drunk on sleep, mind failing to process his setting, and stumbled towards his door. "Daniel, sorry I had to wake you up but it's time to start your day", His mother said, eyes narrowing at his crumpled clothing suggesting that she wasn't so sorry at all. His mother widened the gap, revealing a neat stack of revision books resting on her left arm, Daniel instinctively looked behind him at a pile of battered revision books he had already accumulated and sighed, "Are those really necessary?"

His mother blinked. "I think you already know the answer to that question," she answered, barrelling past him and into his room, wrinkling her nose as her eyes surveyed his retreat, "You should clean your room seeing as you'll be staying here for so long"

Daniel jumped, "How long?" His mother ignored his question, instead occupying herself with placing the revision books onto Daniel's already cluttered desk, pens and dishes strewn haphazardly around his keyboard, only complemented by the deep scratches that ordained the surface, whispering of misuse.

"You can come down and have breakfast, and then you can begin your studies, now that you have the books and the time" his mother commented as she pivoted from his desk and walked out of his room, leaving Daniel staring at the hopeless pile of revision books that had joined the clutter on his desk. Suddenly, yesterday's events rushed over him like a wave, inspiring an ardent curiosity to ignite within Daniel. He scanned his floor for the coin he had used yesterday and saw it, nestled in a discarded jumper, its surface glinting as if winking, letting Daniel in on a secret. He reached for the coin, held it between his fingers, excitement overwhelming scepticism, and flipped it into the air guessing heads. After the coin had finished its elegant airborne twirl, it landed solidly on heads.

Daniel smirked in mild surprise but remained unimpressed, instead powering on his computer, standing rather than sitting in order to look over the new tower of books that had occupied his desk. Navigating to his files, Daniel finally found what he was looking for, a simple Python document that he had coded a while ago, which would return a random value between 1 and 1000. Running the file did not require an internet connection, useful as Daniel no longer had access to his router as per his mother's plan to reform him, and he was faced with a prompt to press enter. Before listening, Daniel chose a number – 552 and then slammed his finger down on Enter. The program immediately returned a value and Daniel paused, eyes staring at the number given. 552. Wondering if it was just a crazy coincidence, Daniel reran the program, this time guessing 999 before pressing enter. Right again – 999. Daniel couldn't believe it. Still lacking conviction, he brought up the raw code and changed some values. Now the program would return a number between 1 and 10,000,000. Daniel breathed in and guessed 52,964. This was it. The evidence that would solidify Daniel's power. Finger hovering above the enter button, Daniel finally brought it down. A microsecond passed, and the result was printed on the screen. 52,964. Fifty-two thousand nine hundred and sixty-four. Daniel was speechless, and an uncontrollable grin twitched across his face. He had powers. "Daniel, are you eating or not?!" his mother's voice called from downstairs, waking him from his victorious stupor. Daniel practically floated downstairs, ate breakfast, used the bathroom and then confined himself to his room leaving his mother perplexed by his eagerness for solitude. Once inside, Daniel changed out of his clothes, still covered in dust from the abandoned house, and went back to his computer.

The program was still running with 52,964 proudly displayed on the screen, and the option to rerun the program blinking enticingly. Unable to resist experimenting with his new ability, Daniel obliged, guessing the number one before hitting enter. The result baffled Daniel. He was wrong. Instead of one being printed onto the screen, it was nine. Maybe he didn't have abnormal luck and the guesses were naturally lucky. Text suddenly began to appear under the unexpected output to Daniel's immense surprise, there was no code that allowed the program to output text. Daniel's mind immediately jumped to malware, strange, as his antivirus would have removed it. The text continued to trickle across his screen, until finally ending. The short paragraph mocking the list of numbers that Daniel's code was limited to returning.

```
Oh, I forgot to mention, even
though you can change probability to
favour you, you can't increase it to
100%. If you're unlucky enough to have
your probability fail, then it will
reduce to its natural state. To regain
your probability, just flip coins.
Simple.
```

While Daniel had his doubts about receiving an ability, it was the output that broke the rules of his code that won him over, something completely impossible with the three lines of code that constructed the output. Daniel powered off his computer, satisfied with his discovery. Now feeling motivated, he collected the various mugs, utensils and plates from his desk and brought them downstairs into the kitchen. The rest of the house smelt different, fresher and cleaner than the smell that Daniel had grown accustomed to, enclosed in his room.

As Daniel passed the living room, he curiously glanced inside, drawn by the sound of the television to see his mother reclined on the couch watching a movie, the changes in lighting from the television clearly visible over her face and the occasional cries and gunfire blasting from the speakers collaborating with the widening of her eyes. Even though it was dark in the living room, the hallway light was on, and as Daniel passed, his mother pounced, "Daniel!". Daniel closed his eyes; would she berate or congratulate him? He hoped she would be happy with his proactivity and as he opened his eyes once more, his mother delivered her answer, "I'm proud that you've finally started cleaning after yourself Dan", surprising Daniel, especially with her use of his shortened name, reserved for good moods only. He looked over to her figure, but she had already gone back to staring at the television, eyes glazed over as she subconsciously sipped from a mug cradled in her hands. Daniel continued his walk to the kitchen where he made sure to deposit his load into the dishwasher, avoiding any further negative confrontation with his mother. After ransacking the cupboards for some snacks, Daniel retrieved a forgotten packet of digestives and headed back to his room. Once inside, Daniel lifted the revision books off his desk, thumping them down onto the floor, uncaring for their integrity and leaving his desk relatively clean. Daniel now had an unobstructed view of his screen. Instead of turning his computer back on, however, Daniel picked up his coin from where it had landed on his unmade bed earlier and sat in his chair, legs propped onto the empty space left on his desk, flipping the coin with one hand while cramming biscuits into his mouth with the other, determined to improve his probability.

His phone vibrated; it was Jesse. Daniel caught his coin, heads – right on his guess, and swiped his screen, accepting the call. "Yo Danny" Jesse began "Sorry for sounding mad at you yesterday – earlier – this morning – doesn't matter, I was just tired"

"I know man, my fault for calling so late" Daniel replied, feeling guilty for forgetting about his friend in the face of his own ecstasy. "So, are you going to tell me what happened yesterday?" Jesse tentatively asked. Daniel hesitated, narrating the events to himself. He sounded crazy, but he hoped Jesse would believe him, being his childhood friend, supporting Daniel when he would come painted blue and purple with bruises from the bullies that seemed to lurk at every corner.

Daniel took a deep breath and told Jesse everything. Occasionally interrupted by a gasp, Daniel stumbled through his recount of the events not missing a single detail. By the time he had finished, the line was silent, leaving Daniel listening to the blood pounding in his ears and the faint static emitted from the speakers. Just as Daniel thought he had made a mistake, his friend burst out cheering, words lost in Daniel's own happiness that his friend had believed him, "Bro, you have got to show me this!"

Daniel scratched his head "I can't, I'm grounded, remember?" He heard a snort come from the other line. "Mate, you have superpowers, use them!" Daniel glanced at the time, reminding him it was 5 pm. "Yeah, alright then, let's meet at the park, there's no way I'm going back to that house."

"Hear hear!" His friend's voice escaped as Daniel ended the call and put his phone on his desk. He racked his brain for what he could use his ability on. He did not doubt that his probability was already high, but Daniel winced, remembering his ability's failure on his Python program, if it failed again when he tried it on his mum, he shuddered to think what fresh horror might fall onto him. Daniel got up, stalked to his bedroom door, and paused, his hand resting on the rough plywood panelling of the door. Internally, Daniel was begging, pleading with his power to work, to let his mother be sufficiently distracted to allow him to sneak outside. Without waiting a second longer, Daniel overcame his hesitation, pushed open his door, and began the first of thirty steps that would take him through the front door, padding softly and avoiding the creaky floorboards.

Daniel reached the opening which led to the living room and timidly peered around the corner. The television was still on, playing what seemed to be a wildlife documentary as Daniel's eyes landed on his mother, the narrator's rich voice seemingly describing what Daniel saw, "...here we have a rare animal in its natural habitat". She was sprawled on the couch heavily sleeping, mouth shamelessly open. Daniel silently pumped his fist and gave his head a thankful pat before leaping over the gap, towards the front door. Once he slipped on his shoes, he flung open the front door and rushed out.

The sky was a breathtaking blue and cloudless, the wind playfully ruffling Daniel's hair. Even though he hadn't stayed inside for longer than usual, with his solace in having an internet connection removed, it was refreshing to finally step outside the house. As Daniel walked towards his rendezvous with Jesse, he felt a sense of euphoria wash over him. No longer was he afraid of eye contact with those he passed on the sidewalk, no longer was he slouched over in a sad attempt to avoid attention. He felt powerful for the first time outside a videogame or political argument, knowing that with the odds in his favour, he could basically do anything.

Distracted by his feeling of superiority, Daniel arrived at the park before he realised it, walking down one of the paths when he saw his friend, who looked like he had barely left his house with shoes on, let alone proper clothing. Jesse wore a crumpled t-shirt, coupled with a pair of trousers that looked suspiciously like his pyjamas. No wonder Jesse had arrived before Daniel, it looked like he had abandoned everything he was doing to see Daniel's power. Walking up to each other, the pair high-fived, leaving Jesse excitedly glancing at his hand "I hope I've got powers now" grinning at Daniel's unamused face. Daniel took out his coin "Jesse, make a guess: heads, or tails?" his friend instinctively replied "Tails!", and Daniel flipped. Once again, Daniel's vision was captured by the elegant spin of the 2 pence in the air, the vibrant blue and green from the surrounding environment clashing with the suborn copper hue of the coin. It fell into his palm and showed it to Jesse. Tails. Jesse opened his mouth to speak but was interrupted by Daniel who raised his finger, signalling him to be patient, and flipped it again and again. Each time the coin fell from its flight, it landed on tails. By the thirtieth flip, Daniel decided that Jesse's eyes were wide enough and broke the silence "Pretty cool, huh?", Jesse nodded, "I ran it on the Python code that we had to write for that homework-"

"And you got it right every time?" Jesse finished, still gaping at the coin resting in Daniel's palm. "Not exactly..." Daniel recounted the failure of his power, "I can't make the probability of something happening 100%." Jesse's face barely fell at the news, he wasn't listening, instead he was wracking his brain for ideas "Danny... why don't we go to the casino? You could make us rich!" his eyes lit up and a grin splayed itself across his face, "My brother works at one, and he could get us in". Daniel, smiled, keen to use his powers in a practical environment and senses blunted by the idea of easy money - "I'm in."

Experimentation

The duo loitered in the park talking and preparing for what would be Daniel's first chance to profit from his ability. Moving from walking, to occupying the swings as Jesse called his brother to secure an entrance to the casino, initially leaving various passive-aggressive voicemails before finally getting through. After some intense haranguing, Jesse finally signalled to Daniel that they were good to go, and hours after Daniel had first left his home, they stood outside the not-so-grand, 'Grand Casino', cheap lights bearing down on the duo, hiding the peeling paint and fading signage. Approaching the entrance, they were greeted by a bouncer, looming over the both of them, his suit barely doing anything to disguise his massive stature and his mirrored sunglasses hiding any hint of humanity from the bristling figure blocking the entrance. However, as they drew to a stop, the bouncer nodded and moved to the side, raising an arm, gesturing to the casino within.

Once inside, the pair were assaulted by the cheap cologne and classic music, too quiet to enjoy but too loud to ignore. The air was heavy with desperation and loss as Daniel's eyes wandered to various figures sitting slumped and defeated or frantically buying more chips to continue gambling. Jesse, who seemed worryingly experienced for someone not normally allowed into a casino, had already begun moving to a row of slot machines, beckoning to Daniel to follow. There were a few people already occupying the machines, some mindlessly pulling on the lever, spinning the icons over and over, in hopes that their losses will be covered by a big win, some slamming the glass shouting, begging for better luck. Daniel felt uncomfortable surrounded by clear despair of people trapped in the cycle of gambling, however he brushed this off when Jesse patted the seat he was to sit in, feeding the machine with bank notes, and stepping back allowing Daniel to work his magic.

Daniel tilted his head and focused on the machine, the odds, and pulled the lever downwards. The flashing lights and goofy sounds entrapped Daniel's attention as the symbols on each of the panels spun into strong primary colours. As the spinning slowed, Daniel's heart rate picked up, and then, a golden seven in the first column, another one in the second and then, finally, after teasing Daniel with failure, a seven in the third row. Immediately the machine's lights oscillated with vibrant yellow, and its speakers erupted into a fanfare of trumpets, announcing Daniel's win. Jesse jumped onto Daniel's back, shouting in delight. However, the other spectators swivelled their attention onto Daniel, the newcomer. The air buzzed with distrust and some even got out of their seats to approach Daniel, bearing faces mutilated by jealousy and suspicion. Jesse glanced behind him at the gathering crowd and pulled Daniel off his seat. The machine was still blaring its victory tune, attracting more players to the pair, until they were both completely surrounded by the glaring, dead eyes of those who had lost everything to gambling, silently shifting positions like zombies at they watched their meal.

Two casino employees pushed themselves through the inanimate crowd of spectators, distinguished by the crimson suits and name tags they wore, eyes widening in surprise when they saw the winner. Instead of congratulating them, they beckoned to them to follow, not looking behind to see if they were following as they stalked to the reception desk. The bright lights in the casino seemed to have become much less welcoming, reflecting the grim faces of the casino workers watching the duo approach the main desk. "Do you have an ID?" an elderly woman asked, her golden badge naming her Laurice Loncoth – General Manager. Presenting the audience of unimpressed casino workers with pointless fumbling of pockets, Jesse finally admitted "We don't have ID.". A smirk flickered across the Manager's face, and she turned to look at a nearby worker both sharing the same conspiring smile, "Sorry, no ID no reward", she leaned in, "and I bet you aren't eighteen either." She stepped away drinking in Jesse's clear expression of horror and protest, ignoring Daniel's apathy. "Security!" She called as she walked back to the staff area, "escort those two to the exit", prompting jeering and chuckling from the audience of casino customers still watching them, glad that Daniel's win had not been 'stolen' from them. The employees dispersed leaving Daniel and Jesse to be frogmarched by the same bouncer that had allowed them to enter in the first place. Once outside, the bouncer patted Jesse's shoulder in solace and entered the casino leaving them outside in the dark.

The sick feeling in Daniel's stomach ebbed away as he breathed in air free of acute desperation and addiction. Looking over to Jesse, it appeared he was concerned with nothing else than getting the winnings "You won that! And they took it from us!"- Daniel noted at his use of "us" as Jesse continued, throwing his arms in the air in anger, where the glint of a streetlight reflected off his watch, reminded him to check the time. Jesse swore. "It's nine, my mum's going to cook me alive", all his anger evaporating immediately, replaced by the expression of a lost, afraid boy, "It's alright anyways, you can do what you did anytime, right?" Without giving Daniel a chance to answer, he nodded to himself and ran off.

Watching, his friend run reminded Daniel of his own situation – he was supposed to be grounded! Taking out his phone, Daniel held his breath, expecting to see a double figure of missed calls from his mother... but there were none. Still, it was late, and Daniel doubted he would be lucky enough to have his absence unnoticed, and so, inspired by Jesse's urgency, Daniel too began running back to his home. As Daniel vaulted over the low wall enclosing his front garden, he noticed that none of the lights were on, strange. But it gave Daniel hope that his mother was still asleep, and it was this belief that spurred Daniel to open the front door quietly, thanking it for its well-oiled hinges and stepped inside. Daniel awkwardly removed his shoes and crept to the dark living room, breathing a sigh of relief as his eyes picked out his mother, still asleep and swaddled in darkness, her face no longer illuminated by the television which had since turned itself off due to inactivity. Daniel let his brow unfurrow in relief and padded upstairs to his room, where he changed into his nightwear and flung himself onto his bed, where his disappointment wrestled with sleep.

Daniel woke up the next morning to the aroma of a hearty breakfast: eggs, toast, and sausages from what Daniel's sleepy senses could distinguish. His eyes snapped open as he probed his completely empty stomach, he had forgotten to eat yesterday. Practically salivating he sat up, his blanket struggling to keep him restrained and galvanised by the smell, levitated downstairs. On the kitchen table were two plates filled with food, visibly smoking. Daniel quickly inserted himself into his seat, waiting for his mother to turn from the oven, where she was preparing some eggs, nearly given away by a ravaging growl from his stomach. Daniel judged by the smell and fizzing. "Oh, good morning, Daniel! I was wondering when you would wake up." his mother exclaimed as she turned around carrying a pan with some eggs which she deposited onto Daniel's plate. His mother then took a seat, and after a short prayer, began to eat. "Did you notice me asleep yesterday, Daniel?" his mother began, startling Daniel from his desperate eating,

"Uh, no - I was in my room the entire day". his mother squinted at Daniel's head as he continued to bury himself into his breakfast.

"You didn't come downstairs to eat or anything?" Silence ensued as Daniel was unable to answer, mouth full with food.

"I had food upstairs" he obviously lied, the animalistic desperation with which he ate causing his mother to frown. Instead of pursuing her inquiry, she turned to her plate, just as Daniel finished ravaging his last two eggs, their golden blood leaking onto his plate. Daniel stood up, finished with his meal, and left the plate in the sink as he wiped his mouth. As he left the kitchen he caught his mother's suspicious gaze, "I'm just hungry because I'm growing", he justified himself weakly, and he knew it too, leaving the kitchen before his mother could probe him.

Daniel made his way back to his room and texted Jesse asking if he got home all right. His phone buzzed almost immediately with Jesse's response "Yea" and then – his phone began vibrating, Jesse was calling. "Hey Danny, I have an idea, let's try your power on some scratch cards. I'll buy and deliver them to you,"

"Uh ok" Daniel responded, still slightly traumatised by the experience in yesterday's casino.

"I'll get the cards to your house in about ten minutes,

and I'll text you when I'm outside, alright?"
Daniel glanced at his clock, "That's fine, see you"
"Bye".

Daniel put his phone down, and picked up his coin, subconsciously flipping it as he thought about his 'power'. Daniel wasn't sure if he enjoyed dabbling in the world of gambling, he saw what it had done to people at the casino, turning them into husks of humans, zombies. However, Daniel wanted the money, not just for himself, but also for Jesse, thinking back to his longing when he showed him the coin flips, and knowing that Jesse lived in a council estate and was always looking for money. Daniel remembered how Jesse would often resort to stealing when he was younger and sell snacks to school children for a profit. However, Daniel knew that he never kept the money for himself, Daniel was the only one Jesse told about what he actually did with the money. He gave it to his parents. Even when Jesse was teased by many for being 'poor' Jesse was still one of the kindest people Daniel knew. So, if he were to use his power, it would be for Jesse.

A vibration from his phone disturbed Daniel from his thoughts - Jesse was here. His mind immediately switched to his mother, what would she think if she saw all those scratch cards on the mat? Daniel's face paled as he heard the clink of the letter box as Jesse pushed the cards through and imagined her thinking she was some sort of gambling, drug-addicted monster. Daniel raced out of his room, not knowing whether she heard the delivery or not, crying "I'll get it!". There on the faded welcome mat lay a bundle of cards, crudely kept together by a rubber band, the bright enticing colours of the cards, contrasting with the homely rug that it sat on. Daniel scooped the cards up just as his mother entered the hallway, confused, "What was it?"

"Oh- nothing, I must've heard something", Daniel replied, tucking the cards into the elastic of his trousers and showing her both his empty hands. His mother nodded and glanced out the window, before retreating back into the living room.

Daniel ran back upstairs, closing and locking his door once he had entered the safety of his room. He tore off the elastic, releasing a disorientating array of colourful scratch cards onto his bed, all of which promised to have a 'Mega Prize!' or a sum larger than £50,000 if scratched correctly. Life-changing money. Daniel fished out his coin and began scratching, calling upon his luck to get a big win. However, as Daniel scratched, he noticed he was not getting the same rush he did when he used his power and that for every scratch card win, he tallied at least another two losses. Scratch after scratch blurred into each other, until Daniel reached for the next one to only receive a fistful of blanket. He had scratched every card. Finally looking around, Daniel blinked; his 'win' pile was dwarfed by the mountain of losing cards, and his largest win was £10 on a £2 scratch card. Perhaps his powers had failed again? Daniel quickly sent a message to Jesse, with the pictures of the scratch cards to prove his defeat. However, as Daniel hit send, he realised why he was unable to improve the probability of receiving a good scratch card – the odds were already set in stone, it was impossible to change the value of a scratch card after he had received it, and since Jesse bought them, there was no guarantee that he had picked the winning cards. Daniel imagined Jesse's frustration, so far Daniel had not made them rich as Jesse had wanted, evident through the entrepreneurial glint in his eyes when Daniel first revealed his powers.

Looking back at his phone, Daniel noticed that Jesse had responded with a sad emoji, followed seconds later by a two-word question: "Casino again?". Before Daniel could reply, surprised that Jesse would even want to return after their last experience, Jesse called him. "Listen Danny, before you say anything, we're going to go to a different casino, buy some fake facial hair and use ID that's not ours. I'll use my brother's."
Daniel hesitated. "The only ID I can use is my dad's"
There was a pause on the other line as Jesse realised that his eagerness had overtaken him, "Listen man, I'm sorry-"
"I know you are, everybody and their extended family made that clear" Daniel barked, gritting his teeth in grief.

His father's funeral was two months ago, and yet the memory of begging him to stay alive still plagued him, the funeral and the sea of black shirts the chorus of sniffles and teary eyes surrounding him after it had been found that Daniel's pleading fell on deaf – dead- ears, the yellowed hand he had clutched on the bedside was lifeless. Reeled back into his memory Daniel remembered how he stood overlooking the grave, eyes dry, numbed to the core. His father was his mentor, his confidant, his restraint and when he was wrenched away by cancer, he left a gaping hole in his family. His mother was distraught but was forced to fit into her husband's shoes, leaving her with no time to grieve, resulting in the distancing of Daniel's family. Daniel was given greater responsibility and a minimal margin for error.

But then Daniel remembered Jesse and realised how selfish he was. Jesse needed money, the financial sinkhole his family was trapped in was worse than it was in secondary school, and if they did not get help, their family might fragment just like Daniel's. Daniel vaguely remembered the subject of most arguments between his parents being money, and Daniel did not want Jesse to experience that. "I'm sorry Jesse"
"It's fine bro, let me figure it out for yo-"
"I'm going to use my dad's driver's license" Daniel interrupted, heart already set on helping Jesse.

"What? Are you sure?" Jesse incredulously asked.

"Yes."

Daniel could hear the excited grin in Jesse's voice, as encouraged by Daniel he continued, "Alright then tomorrow after lunch, we should have time to get the fake hair and get through some Casino games."

"Deal"

"Alright, see you"

"Bye."

    Daniel ended the call and fell spread-eagled onto his bed, releasing a suppressed exhalation. To his knowledge his father's driver's license was in his room, which had become more of a time capsule after his death. The only thing changed was his bed, which was remade after his dad's removal. Daniel remembered watching it from a sort of third-person perspective, the heart-wrenching cries of his mother as she clawed at the paramedics removing his father, fading into a background din as Daniel let his hand slip from his father's receding arm. Days later, his mother had entered the lifeless room in the morning and had not left until late into the evening, leaving the room in a state of eerie cleanliness. Every detail arranged perfectly to transform the room into something closer to a shrine, however neither he nor his mother had gone inside since that day, visiting the room only in memory.

Daniel stood before the door to his father's room. It had become his father's after he had become sick, inheriting a guest room to allow for monitoring apparatuses to be installed, accommodating for his extra needs. Daniel reached for the brass doorknob, skin protesting against its bone cold bite; hand failing to react, Daniel twisted the knob, the sound of the springs turning breaking the deathly, almost tangible silence that had enveloped the house, as if it too was holding its breath. Daniel pushed the door open remaining outside the room, rooted in place, as the room was slowly revealed by the door's lazy swing. The cold air that rushed out to Daniel and pulled him stung his warm skin, as if hungry for warm, living blood. Daniel looked around, subconsciously shivering as goosebumps erupted onto his skin, the room was devoid of colour as well as life.

The books that his father had proudly collected over the years had lost their vibrancy, as if the only person who gave them meaning took their lives when he lost his. White, pristine sheets, corroborated with the bone white of the walls which barely contrasted with the washed array of colours belonging to the protruding spines of the books. The room was sterile like a hospital ward and so crisp – sharp, that Daniel feared his hand would draw blood if he touched even the impossibly straightened blanket, devoid of even a suggestion of previous use. Creaseless, spotless, lifeless. The sole window overlooking the bed was closed, draped with a shroud of opaque curtains that strangled the sunlight, filtering it into a dreary, depressed light that barely illuminated the dust that had carpeted this bodiless tomb. Daniel finally blinked as he remembered the reason for his intrusion into the room reserved for death. His dad's credentials. Unwilling to wait anymore, Daniel crept across the room towards the bedside cabinet, wading through the stagnant air.

On the cabinet stood a framed picture of his father, Daniel had almost forgotten what he had looked like, remembering instead a blurry figure of warmth and happiness. The portrait was encased in a matte silver frame, a coffin for a printed memory of his father. Daniel tugged at the top drawer, which was stuck from the lack of use, until it gave way with an annoyed groan, revealing his dad's brown leather wallet, worn around the edges, just like Daniel remembered. Picking it up, Daniel closed his eyes imagining he had been given it by his father, his smell still clinging to the leather and Daniel could almost see him, arms outstretched until Daniel opened his eyes and he disappeared. Instead, he remembered the stench of essential oils, medicine and sweat that pervaded the room during his father's last hours and with his subdued memories coming back to life, Daniel rushed from the room, closing the door as he left, once again sealing the tomb. Daniel leaned backwards onto the door and flipped open the wallet, washed with a sense of relief when revealed was his father's driver's license and a couple of forgotten bank notes. Snapping it shut, Daniel retreated into his room and deposited the wallet on his desk, ready to be used tomorrow.

CASINO HEIST

The next morning Daniel woke up and sat up in a fluid motion, eyes immediately darting towards his desk where he had left the wallet. His shoulders sagged with relief when his sleepy eyes finally distinguished the dark brown square of the wallet from the camel-coloured desk it slept on, catalysed with furious eye-rubbing. He had been afraid that the wallet, now the closest thing that Daniel had to his dad, had disappeared, since his life seemed to be becoming increasingly spontaneous and unpredictable. Picking up his phone, Daniel noticed a message from Jesse reminding him about their plans. ID. Disguise. Casino.

Daniel pushed his blanket off him and crawled out of bed, barely conscious as he dressed into his clothes, thinking about the money he could make from the casino, and how it would not only help Jesse and his family, but also him. He imagined the luxury he could buy, when as he was about to put his last hand through his t-shirt sleeve, he stopped himself, afraid of being too hopeful. He palmed his father's wallet and grabbed his coin, before padding downstairs to find the kitchen empty. Glancing at the clock, Daniel was mildly surprised at his unusual sleep-in, it was ten o'clock. His mother would have already left for work, and glancing through a driveway-facing window, his suspicions were confirmed, she was gone. Daniel made himself a bowl of cereal absentmindedly as he instead focused on the surface of the coin, procrastinating the moment that he would have to closer examine his father's wallet.

The head of two pence bore a sideways portrait of Elizabeth II staring to Daniel's left, where he was attempting to manoeuvre the cereal box over his bowl with one hand, operating through just his peripheral vision and a faction of his attention. Flipping over the coin, Daniel observed the grooves that were meant to mark the edge of the coin were worn smooth from the constant exchanges it had endured. The emblazoned text on the tail end of the coin declared it to be made in 1955, writing that Daniel could only read with the help of the sunlight streaming in from the window behind him and by tilting the coin, a testament to its service. As Daniel observed the coin, his left hand continued to prepare his breakfast, moving on to milk, however as he squinted at the coin, he continued to pour milk, which had begun to overflow from the bowl and edge towards Daniel.

Finally satisfied with his scrutiny, Daniel brought the coin down but immediately raised it again, rearing in surprise, as looking down for a spot to place the coin, he no longer saw the table but an advancing stream of milk. In that same fluid motion, Daniel raised the carton of milk, which was still steadily draining, and left its now empty shell in a puddle of its contents. Daniel promptly stood up, letting his wooden chair clatter onto the hard, tiled kitchen floor, hurriedly tearing a handful of kitchen towels from a nearby roll and pressed them against the spillage, leaving his coin on a dry part of the table as he used both his hands to apply the towels.

As he cleaned up the mess, he felt his phone in his trouser pocket begin vibrating warning Daniel of an incoming call. Jesse. With both hands still occupied, Daniel looked up at the time, and allowed his heart rate to slow down, he still had time until he met with Jesse. But the vibrating barely stopped before it resumed. Daniel absorbed the final patch of milk and threw the sodden towels into the bin before finally dragging his phone from his pocket with damp hands. Without verifying the caller, Daniel answered the phone and pressed it to his ear, "Yes?"

"Daniel, I won't be able to come today" Jesse, urgently murmured, his sisters' background giggling audible over his friend's whispers "I'll transfer you £20, it should cover your costs and let you play a few games, sorry I can't talk, I'll call you later on."

"Uh, ok" Daniel answered, bemused by his friend's uncharacteristic seriousness, "Bye."

"Bye."

The call ended with a beep that allowed Jesse's words to wash over Daniel like unwanted torrential downpour. He would have to go on his own. The only experience Daniel had with casinos was his brief visit but that was enough to deter him from ever wanting to enter another one, Jesse, however, had snuck into casinos throughout his years with the help of his older brother who ricocheted around casinos as a bouncer.

Regardless of reluctancy, Daniel's concern for Jesse motivated him. He put his phone away and finished his breakfast, avoiding the distracting glimmer of the coin basking in the morning light, trying to stay focused on his preparation. Even though Jesse had transferred him £20, Daniel wanted to keep it for the casino so he could get him the best return on investment he could. Daniel deposited his empty bowl in the sink, aware that it would annoy his mother, but he was unwilling to delay any longer. Shrugging on his jacket, Daniel glanced at the clock before leaving the confines of his home, he had until seven o'clock until she arrived back home from work, eight at best, if she stayed behind finishing a spreadsheet or whatever accountants did. It occurred to Daniel that he barely knew anything about his mother's job, one that she was forced to take after his father's death to keep the bills paid and food on the table. As Daniel walked down the almost desolate pavement towards the commercial area, he resolved to interest himself more in his mother's work and perhaps even provide enough money with his ability that she would not have to work anymore.

Daniel rounded the corner onto the Highstreet, immediately met by throngs of people milling about, having to stop abruptly as the couple in front paused to peer through the window of a toy store. Continuing down the street Daniel noticed an ATM, nearly walking past when he realised, he did not have cash on him. He to cut the path of a jogger as he spontaneously pivoted towards the ATM, fiddling with it for a couple seconds before stepping away, pocket holding four five pound notes. Now ready to continue his quest, Daniel craned his neck to look over the heads of people searching for the store sign he was looking for. There. The costume shop, literally named 'Disguise!'. Daniel had always been interested by its erratic lettering and striking costumes on display, of which were rotated from the store front and were replaced by others every week. However, Daniel finally had an excuse to enter the store, and after nearly hitting a cyclist while crossing the road, he pushed through the opaque, green-tinted door, triggering a distant bell, and stepped inside.

From the outside, the store appeared to be dwarfed by two multinational stores, but one inside its dimensions seemed to multiply. Racks upon racks of colourful, monotone, patterned, plain fabrics surrounded Daniel almost immediately. Outfits upon outfits, topped with wigs of extreme shapes, sizes and colours; top hats, fedoras, propeller beanies, or just regular baseball caps were just a few of the hats Daniel could distinguish, perched on every edge like inquisitive parrots, leaning over to look at the visitor. Daniel pushed himself through the ludicrous skirts of an elegant dress of which intruded into the pathway between racks of clothes, practically screaming Disney princess.

The deeper Daniel explored into the store, the more dense and extreme the clothing became until walking seemed more like wading through the invasive arrangements of fabric, reaching for him like the greedy stretching vines in a jungle holding its breath in the presence of an apex predator. Finally squeezing past a comically oversized suit, Daniel was presented with a corner stolen from Specsavers. The wall was of exposed wood expelling a homely vibe, with holes to hold the frames of the hundreds of glasses. Continuing the erratic theme were several glasses of various proportions. One pair had perfectly square lenses whereas another had what looked like a hollow honeycomb for each of the lenses. There was a pair of glasses for every colour, a thought that solidified in Daniel's mind as he continued to gaze at the array of spectacles in search of a pair he could use.

Daniel pulled out his father's wallet in hopes of inspiration, leather creaking as he opened it to extract the driver's license from behind the clear plastic that held it in place. Examining it, Daniel realised his mistake, of course his father was not wearing his glasses in the picture - he was not supposed to. While this gave Daniel ample opportunity to select even the most bizarre of glasses he still felt drawn to finding glasses of resemblance to his father's horn-rimmed ones that he often wore, and as he skimmed over tens of options his eyes landed on what appeared to be the more sensible side of the shelving, offering glasses you could wear to work and not just to amuse yourself in front of your bedroom mirror, hidden away from inquisitive eyes. Although Daniel had limited his search to a fraction of the wall, the sheer volume of glasses meant he had to keep track with his finger in order to stop his eyes from jumping to the next interesting pair of glasses before his brain had finished processing.

As he ticked off several pairs, his finger finally stopped on a pair of horn-rimmed, circular glasses almost identical to those of his father. Daniel stooped and carefully plucked them from their relatively low perch and put them on, glancing at a convenient mirror only to feel a jolt of recognition. These were the ones. Once Daniel had taken them off, he gave his father's driver's license a quick glance before deciding the facial hair he would need to buy. However, looking around, Daniel could not see shelves selling anything but clothing and accessories and standing still surrounded by volume-dampening material, he grew aware of just how quiet it was in the store. After all, it was probably midday by now, and even though Daniel doubted the store's popularity, he wondered whether there should be a group of kids off school messing about in here.

Unable to continue standing surrounded by the deafening silence, Daniel cried "Hello?", his voice dulled by the natural acoustic of the store, drowning what Daniel had hoped to be a shrill ring for assistance instead into a flat and heavy murmur. But just as Daniel opened his mouth again, a rustle to his right announced a body pushing itself through a dense row of clothing, finally revealing a wizened woman. Her face was so defined by winkles that they looked artificial. The hexagonal glasses perched on the bridge of her nose magnifying her grey eyes, containing them behind her spectacles like goldfish in a fishbowl. However, several wrinkles joined the mass already prominent on her face as she smiled, "How may I help you?"

Daniel fumbled with his father's driver's license, bringing it before him for her massive eyes to land on. "Do you have a moustache that looks like this?", Daniel shifted his finger to point at his father's top upper lip, but the shop assistant had already moved her eyes back to Daniel, ignoring his squirms of discomfort, "Yes, of course! Please follow me."

The woman, surprisingly agile for her age swivelled on her heel and marched back into the jungle of clothing, leaving Daniel scrambling after her. His guide took several turns before finally pulling back hangers of multi-coloured suits, blemished by brazen batches and fearless polka dots, to reveal a hidden shelf packed with enough facial hair to fill a mattress in plastic wrapping. Without waiting for Daniel to absorb the scene, the woman extracted a bag and handed it to a bemused Daniel. "I- uh- is this the right one?" he asked, bringing the bag to eye level, examining the content.

"Of course it's the right one" the assistant replied in an exasperated tone, "I will be at the check-out", she murmured before her bulbous eyes glazed over, briefly staring at an empty space on the ceiling before breaking from the daydream and muttering something about a cat before plunged back into the jungle of clothing, leaving Daniel standing awkwardly clutching a bag of fake facial hair and staring at the back of her rapidly receding lime cardigan.

    Realising that he would have to navigate the maze to pay and exit, he promptly began in the same direction as the woman had left in, shrugging the sleeves of various pieces of attire that clung to his body as he pushed through. Daniel had hoped to reach one of the store's walls and gain his bearings from there but his expectations for adventure were stumped when the density with which the clothing was hooked began to expand, thinning out the stuffy texture so many clothes gave the air, and allowing him to make out the fluorescent green of a fire exit sign, that encouraged Daniel and eventually brought him to the check-out. Rather than the Tesco checkout that flashed in Daniel's mind when it was referred to by the shop assistant, he was surprised by an archaically built spruce front desk, shaped like a librarian's desk, complemented by the unnecessarily elevated form of the woman, wide eyes looking down upon Daniel. He dumped the glasses and facial hair on the table, "I'd like to buy these please", leaving the woman to pick up the items and process them. After a few moments, she turned from an obscured screen and offered Daniel his final price, exactly £5. Daniel hesitated briefly, surprised by the absence of the omnipresent beep of barcode scanners in stores that he was used to, and by the cheap price. Daniel paid but as he collected the items, the woman stopped him, "Since you're a new customer you can get a pair of height-adjusting soles for free"

"Ah, yes please." Daniel gratefully accepted, allowing the woman to deposit a see-through baggie containing soles on the small pile of items he was already carrying. "They'll make you a good inch taller, those, perfect for looking completely different," she said winking and Daniel blushed, stammering,

"I-it's for a uh- school project"

"Mhm" was the reply, and judging from the amused smile that pulled lines around her eyes, she knew Daniel's intentions were not innocent. Daniel turned away from the desk only glancing back to wish the woman a good day and followed the directives of arrows on the floor to where the exit lay behind two racks of clothing, and stepped out into the fresh air of the high street where sounds cut through the air like a sharpened knife and every breath brought pleasantly refreshing air into his lungs.

Hearing his footsteps connecting with the grey pavement, Daniel realised it was the first time he heard them since entering the shop, its thick, padded carpet smothering the retort of his trainers against the floor. His phone vibrated multiple times now able to reach the signal that the shop had also deterred, and Daniel tapped on the latest message from Jesse which was sent about the time Daniel had entered the store. Within it were the details of the casino he would be targeting. Mega Emporium was its name; Daniel could almost imagine its brightly illuminated name crowning a sprawling complex, fed by the loss and addiction of its customers, and the soulless, blank faces of the employees honed to encourage consumer spending and minimise casino cost. The casino itself was relatively close to Daniel and the high street, perfect for ensnaring potential victims with cheap lights and superficial smiles. Google Maps quickly directed Daniel off the high street into a spare alley which branched into yet another, finally opening up into a drab street holding unkept-looking bars and shops shuttered closed in defeat, the defiant graffiti desecrating what was left of storefronts. However, as Daniel approached the casino, he began to hear the same classical music that pervaded the first casino, causing Daniel's heart to beat faster as he drew closer, instead of inspiring the relaxing effect normally associated with strings and brass.

It was already dark outside with the sparse sunlight being finally choked by an approaching storm, and it had just begun to pitter-patter with rain when the casino sauntered into Daniel's vision. It squatted on the other side of the road between two bars hoping to reap the rewards from those whose judgement was clouded by alcohol. From Daniel's position he could make out the indent of the casino entrance and two bouncers standing in their trademark black suits, arms crossed, and eyes censored by mirrored sunglasses, regardless of the weather. Daniel entered a small café that, by the looks of it, seemed to be struggling to survive, its empty, rustic wooden tables contrasting with the jeering and laughter of the packed pub across from it. Daniel cursed his lack of foreshadowing as he awkwardly clutched his purchase from 'Disguise!' and approached the front till where a visibly bored teenager sat on her phone. As he came closer, she looked up, face lighting up in pleasant surprise and phone placed – screen down, she was clearly not expecting any customers, "Hi, how may I help you?"

"Hi, do you have any toilets?",

Immediately her face fell, but she quickly covered it up by pointing to a discreet corner, "Of course! Just over there."

"Thank you."

The toilet was spotless, with stainless steel sinks lining one wall and three cubicles lining the other. The floor was made of black marble, useful for hiding stains and scuffs, continuing from the speckled black carpet of the rest of the café. Once inside the cubicle furthest from the door, Daniel locked it with his sleeve and gingerly brought the toilet lid down, minimising contact as much as he could. He sat down, examining his purchase, deciding that he would only put on the soles as he did not wish to be too blatant about his disguise, especially after the girl at the till had already seen his face. Daniel figured that he would need some space to put in the soles and spying the convenient café, he took his chance.

He slipped off his trainers, inserted the soles, and squeezed his feet back in, finding that the space his feet had taken for granted was now compromised. However, as Daniel stood up, he felt the difference, he could now nearly look over the cubicle wall. Daniel grabbed his other accessories and left the cubicle, admiring the difference in height in the mirrors topping the sink. Daniel prayed that the cashier would not notice his change in appearance as he pushed back through the toilet door and made his way back to the front of the store. Instead of the look of confusion and suspicion that Daniel was expecting, the teenager seemed unfazed by his rapid growth, and continued to look at Daniel expectantly. Daniel finally gave in to her hopeful expression and purchased a chocolate muffin before changing his mind, revelling in her childish delight to finally be given something to do. The feeling was dampened as Daniel stepped back onto the street, wincing as he realised, he had wasted Jesse's money.

Approaching Mega Emporium's main entrance, Daniel noticed a convenient cleft in its wall, with a discreet road leading into an area reserved for bins and ducked inside, out of sight of the casino bouncers. Nearly gagging from the rancid smell and the whole muffin he had stuffed into his mouth, Daniel was forced to stand in the middle of the tarmac to avoid the split bin bags that had broken from the industrial dumpsters lining the walls, crept across the pavement and begun consuming the road. Gingerly nudging a bold bin bag backwards, Daniel created enough space to put on his disguise. He tore open the wrapping of his moustache, carelessly discarding it in a pile of bin bags, and stuck it on his upper lip, pressing it down until he felt it was secure enough. He then pulled the plastic horn-rimmed glasses off the neck of his t-shirt and placed them on his head, diving headlong into the sea of anonymity as he straightened his posture, transforming him completely. Even without taking out his phone to examine his appearance, Daniel felt different, but he was slack-jawed when he did.

Looking back at him from his screen was his father, the moustache perfectly imitating the one his father stubbornly groomed and the glasses were a replica of the ones used by his dad to distance himself from the world. Daniel had always had people tell him he looked like his dad, especially after the funeral, but he had shrugged them off as comments to fill in the awkward silence of people afraid to hurt your feelings. Daniel snapped a photo, sent it to Jesse, and powered off his phone. Now fully focused on the casino, Daniel stepped out into the street towards its entrance with steeled nerves and the skin of a different man. Once at the entrance, he flashed his father's driver's license to one of the two burly bouncers completely blocking the Casino's revolving doors from view. After a second's consideration they neatly stepped aside presenting the portal into the world of exploited hope and lost dreams.

Daniel entered the casino with a calm confidence, eyes already darting to the bountiful array of slot machines, poker tables, and roulette wheels whose lights assaulted Daniel's eyes, hoping to draw in a new victim. Answering the call of a near roulette table, Daniel plastered a false smile across his face and strode over, playing with the coin in his pocket as he prepared to unleash his ability. Daniel sat down, sizing up the other two players, one of whom was nursing a large collection of chips painted with the primary, childhood colours of red, yellow and green. The other player sat further away; face masked by his hand while the other nervously fidgeted with two green chips, the only ones Daniel could see he had. The dealer turned to Daniel, their polished, professional face giving nothing away as they asked Daniel what chips he wanted, beckoning to an array of different colours. Daniel pointed to a pile of red chips, inspired by the apparently successful player next to him, "How many?" "How much is one?" Daniel asked, aware of the £10 left in his pocket, decimated by his disguise and the muffin.

"One red is £5." The dealer offered; a glint of curiosity pushing through his mask of indifference.

"I'll take two" Daniel pushed forward his ten pound note, which was snapped up in a rapid blur of movement, replaced by Daniel's two red chips. Meanwhile, the player by Daniel had pushed a neat tower of two red chips onto the number 24, placing his bet. When Daniel looked at him, he received a mischievous smile and a raised eyebrow. A clear challenge. Daniel suppressed a smirk and went all in on number 23, his opponent sitting back in satisfaction. The distant player stood up clutching his meagre winnings, unwilling to lose any more chips, leaving Daniel and the other player in the game. The dealer glanced at the bets and nodded, placing down a black sphere on the wheel before spinning it.

The ball lazily spun around the wooden frame of the wheel, pinned by Daniel's eyes as he willed it to land on 23. The ball finally began to lose its momentum, dipping down onto the spinning wheel, the clash in velocity sending the ball into the air where it arced for a fraction of a second before clattering down, swept away by the wheel. The number it landed on was hidden by the wall of the roulette wheel for a second before emerging as the carousel of odds continued. Number 23. Daniel controlled the grin that began to rip across his face and glanced at his opponent through his peripheral vision. The man was still leaning back, face contorted into one of disbelief. He had not expected to win when he had bet but had goaded Daniel into betting so he would lose all his money. Daniel's bet on 23, one number away from 24 strengthened the man's clear disbelief. He could tell that from the man's insistent tapping on the carpeted table, he wanted Daniel's attention. However, instead of entertaining the man Daniel stayed focused on the wheel, which had come to a stop, verifying that Daniel had bet against the odds – and won, earning him back his red chips plus an additional two. His opponent's persistent tapping abruptly stopped as he left the game, however rather than walking off to the front desk or 'cage' as it was labelled by signs, to cash in his chips, or to another game, the man remained standing, just outside of Daniel's field of view, spectating.

Slightly unnerved by the man's prolonged presence behind him, Daniel went all in on number one, ready to collect his winnings and move onto another game. Still, the dealer's face revealed no surprise at the brazen act and proceeded to prepare the wheel. Poised with the glossy black ball in the ridge leading it to the main wheel, the dealer spun the roulette, sending it into a lazy spin and making its outcome impossible to predict releasing the ball after a second's wait, its progress downwards towards the wheel marked by the murmur of metal rushing against polished wood. The ball bounced once when it reached the wheel, leaping over three numbers and rolling over a third as its momentum was broken. However, there was no doubt that when it landed on the number one the ball had stabilised and was swept with the rotation of the wheel. Daniel had won again. He momentarily forgot to express the glee anybody in this situation would emit and stood up to accept his winnings from the dealer, nodding in thanks as the dealer, who instead of returning double his red chips, gave him one grey one that Daniel assumed held the same value. Before turning away Daniel deposited his winnings into his pocket, realising that he would need a more permanent solution to store the chips he would inevitably rack up, but decided it to be a problem for his future self as he turned around… coming face to face with his spectator.

Now with an excuse to look at him, Daniel observed his greasy hair, pulled back and gelled to give the facade of elegance. Daniel had smelt the musk that was flowing from the man's tired suit when he had first arrived at the table but assumed it was a cheap, cloying perfume chosen by some out-of-touch higher-up to help customers feel at ease and spend more money within the casino. The man's hands slowly arced as they came together in lazy applause, stopping before they could clap together, "That was impressive." He reached out with his right hand for a handshake, palm glistening with sweat and nails highlighted by black matter that was entrenched behind them - "Do you think you'll be as lucky in poker?"

Daniel ignored the outstretched hand and shrugged "I don't know how to pl-" "So modest, let's go to that table" The man interrupted, pointing a grimy finger towards an empty table, preparing to take a step but stopping himself, when he looked back towards Daniel, giving him a half-hearted smile, "I'm Alan by the way" before turning back towards the table, raising his hand to beckon Daniel onwards.

Alan sat himself on the opposite side of the poker table, keeping the dealer between him and Daniel, clearly looking to play seriously. The dealer spread out, mixed and dealt out the cards sending two to Alan and two to Daniel, leaving three on the centre of the green felt table. Daniel cautiously peeked at his cards, controlling his facial expressions as he lifted them to see a King and a Queen. Daniel did not know how to play poker but knew that he had two of the biggest cards. He glanced up to Alan who was intensely studying Daniel, glancing down when their eyes met. Alan raised, pushing forward three grey chips and Daniel copied, not sure what else he could say and nudged forward all he had: four red and one grey chip. The dealer tutted, "Fold if you can't match his bid," firing Daniel a condescending glare.

Alan looked over, and gasped theatrically, "So sorry...?"

"Daniel." he responded, without thinking.

"I'm so sorry Daniel – here," Alan rolled a grey chip

towards Daniel where it curled neatly into his meagre pile, allowing Daniel to play.

The game continued, however Daniel was no longer focused on the game but on his identity, if his name was corroborated with his father's driver's license, they would find that it did not belong to a Daniel but to a Paul Hochrein. His leg bounced against the floor, and Alan noticed, mistaking his anxiety for bad luck with his cards. The dealer contributed another two cards to the three already sitting at the middle. The added cards were an ace of clubs and a ten of clubs, and judging from Alan's quick eyebrow raise, it was rare.

The cards they joined were a three of hearts a jack of clubs and a two of hearts, cards that remained insignificant to Daniel, who merely noticed that two of the five cards had red lettering. Alan finally flipped his cards, revealing two tens - one of hearts and one of spades, and sat back with a satisfied look washing over his face. In response, Daniel flipped his cards over immediately causing Alan to choke on his spit and stand up, "What?!" his voice cracked. Daniel frowned at him, confused at his erratic behaviour. "That's a-a royal flush!" Even the dealer looked surprised but quickly regained professionalism and brought the chips pooled to Daniel.

SORE LOSERS

As Daniel examined his winnings, Alan, still standing, motioned to someone behind Daniel's field of view and Daniel looked up when three muscular men wearing all-black suits, sewing straining against their bulging muscles, sat down at the same table. Their men-in-black appearance like the bouncers at the casino entrance. All of them were styled with the same greasy hair as Alan, bar one, who was bald, immediately earning the name Bald Guy from Daniel.

They all remained seemingly uninterested in Daniel, failing to extend a hand in greeting or utter a word of acknowledgement, and judging from their physique, these men talked with their muscle not their mouth. The other two were clean-shaven and had the same military cut, glistening in the gold casino light with almost the same ferocity as the naked head of Bald Guy. Although the pair looked like they had been made in a cloning lab, Daniel noticed a difference between them. One had golden teeth, replacing both his front teeth, made visible with every mouth movement as he grinded at a bit of chewing gum. His name was Golden Teeth, and the other one he called Snake Eyes, complimentary of his constantly darting eyes that seemingly never blinked.

Although Daniel assumed they were friends of Alan, he could not help but feel intimidated by the mountains of hulk that had joined the game. Daniel thought that the casino had become quieter following Alan's signal, but he assumed it must be his imagination, still drunk on his win. Daniel tore his eyes away from the men and looked at Alan instead, who met his gaze and held it, eyes cold with silent fury. "Dan, mind if I call you Dan? Do pass my chips back – consider that round a practice round." Missing the dealer's look of disapproval, Daniel shrugged and passed over the chips he had won from Alan. In response, his face relaxed and he exhaled, shoulders visibly untensing, "That was a very lucky game, how about another?"
"Sure."

The dealer retrieved all the cards on the table and reshuffled them, filling the uncomfortable silence with the sound of felt against card. All the players bet, leaving Daniel with no choice but to go all in, the total value of chips reaching the hundreds. Starting with Alan, the dealer dealt the cards, and silence filled the table as each player peeked at their cards in turn. Daniel finally glanced at his and felt his heart hammed when he realised, he had an ace of hearts and a king of hearts. Daniel was set to have another royal flush and considering the cards already on the table – a queen of hearts, a king of clubs and a three of spades, the odds looked to be in Daniel's favour.

As the dealer placed yet another two cards onto the middle of the table, Daniel remained still as the others leaned forward to get a good look. A jack of hearts and a nine of hearts had joined the row, securing Daniel's win. The other players also began to notice the odd number of hearts on the table and Golden Teeth shared a look with Snake Eyes, tapping his cards to imply that he had a good hand. Alan flipped his cards over, exposing a bad hand. Why had he not folded? Alan seemed untroubled by his poor cards, and eagerly looked at Snake Eyes who sat next to him as he flipped over his cards. His face slightly dropped in disappointment when similarly useless cards were revealed.

Golden Teeth was next, struggling to flip over his cards, his sausage fingers struggling to hold onto the edge of them. Snake eyes leaned over until both were scrabbling at the cards as if they were glued to the table. Finally, Alan got out of his seat, visibly exasperated, and stalked to where the duo sat hunched over, almost breaking sweat, and pushed them away, flipping over the cards himself, easily, eyes lighting up when the cards were revealed. Ten of clubs and ten of spades. Daniel assumed that paired with the ten of hearts already on the table centre, that would normally be a great hand. However, rubbing his cards together, Daniel knew that it was nothing compared to what he was about to show them.

Bald Guy flipped his cards over, revealing one of hearts and two of clubs, completing a sequence, but inferior compared to Golden Teeth's hand. Regardless of his hand, Bald Guy joined the others grinning, clearly believing that his group had won the game. Daniel turned his cards over. Another royal flush. Statistically, it was nearly impossible, but Daniel defied the odds, feeling immense satisfaction as he stared around at the table, savouring the smiles wiping off his opponents' faces as each processed the cards and their significance to the cards already on the table. The lights were brighter than ever, and Daniel felt the addictive rush of a gambler after his first big win, as he savoured the mountain of chips that the dealer prepared to give him. The green of the table grew in vibrancy and Daniel wanted to win again, knowing that he would get what he wanted.

As he was absorbed into a euphoria-educed trance, Alan motioned to his men, and Bald guy shifted too fast for Daniel to realise what he was doing until it was too late. A burlap sack engulfed his view, drowning the lucid colours and bringing him back to reality, dragging him from the artificial extravagance of the casino and its false whispers of quick riches and chasing luck.

Daniel reeled backwards pushing himself off the stool and onto the floor, now blind, he relied on his memory to judge his adversaries' positions. "I think he was cheating, sir" Daniel heard the dealer murmur amid the rustling of the sack against his ears, answered by Alan's oiled voice,
"Yes. He thinks we're fools, and for that, he pays."
Daniel desperately scrabbled away from the table, pulling at the sack at the same time, the rough burlap scratching against his neck as it was held in place by a drawstring at its lip that was tightened around his neck, preventing removal.

Even the carpeted casino floor could not muffle the heavy, dramatic footsteps of his approaching attackers so he used his arm as leverage, pushing himself onto it and kicked out with his leg, attempting to sweep their legs from underneath them. However, his attempt to defend himself was futile, a crack jarred his leg as his shin connected with the wood of the poker table, prising a gasp of pain from Daniel's lips. Two sets of rough hands grabbed him from his shoulders and tugged him upwards. "Move him out." It was Alan. His concern with Daniel had malevolent intentions from the beginning, perhaps tipped off by his audacious luck, and thinking back, Alan's mask of friendliness did not fit his face, the anger after he lost was just a hint of lay behind it, and now that it was off, Daniel was experiencing Alan's true personality.

The casino was deathly silent, the minimal hubbub that kept the casino feeling full was absent, the classical music, steadily playing in the background, now gone, replaced by continuous scratching of rough sack over Daniel's face. Faint light shone through sack but not enough to navigate by, a thought punctuated by a stumble as Daniel tripped over a carpeted step as he continued to be manhandled somewhere. How was nobody saying anything? Daniel expected there to be commotion, resistance, help, but there was nothing, almost as if the entire casino was empty, almost as if Daniel had not given the slot machines a nostalgic glance to see them rigidly full of people drunk on the hope of an easy win, big enough to cover their losses. Suddenly it dawned upon Daniel, Alan's signal. Somehow, while Daniel's back was turned the casino must have emptied, leaving just Daniel, Alan and his goons.

The metallic, bitter taste of blood filled Daniel's mouth and he gingerly ran his tongue over his teeth, feeling faint relief when he noted none were missing. Now that the adrenaline was draining, Daniel could feel his right shin throbbing with greater persistence, shooting pain across his body and earning himself a brutal slap across the head as he began limping from his injury. "Keep moving." an anonymous voice demanded, a shove propelling him against the hands restraining his arms.

A door opened; the distant sound of traffic struggled with the shifting sack on Daniel's head, they were outside. The repugnant smell of garbage rushed at Daniel, as he stepped into what had to be a festering bin bag, its juices soaking Daniel's left foot as he plunged his foot through its straining black skin. The jailer clutching his right arm retched as his eyes led him to the exposed contents of bag, nearly crushing Daniel's arm as he lifted him out of the mess and pushed him forwards.

Daniel imagined that they had exited by a side door leading to the overflowing rubbish bins he had avoided as he put his disguise on earlier. But regardless of their obscured position from the rest of the street, the cool air, and the steady sound of a stationary, waiting car ignited something within Daniel, and he reared backwards, attempting to smash the back of his head into and adversary behind him, instead meeting air and receiving a rough backhand for his trouble, "Help! Help -"

A massive hand clamped over Daniel's mouth and at once, a zip tie was cruelly tightened around his wrists and both arms guiding him threw him into a vehicle, head slamming against the opposite door, face pancaked against the seats and hopes vanishing with the final slamming door behind him and the automatic click of locks being enabled.

Daniel lost track of how long they drove, of how many lefts and rights they took, how many stops they did. The first stop was enough to catapult him from his ledge on the padded seats into the footwell, where the window light that had filtered through his sack was gone and where Daniel was hugged by the base of the seats he fell from and the back of the driver's seat, pushing his shoulders backwards. With his vision obscured by the sack he was growing motion sick and with nothing but his imagination to fill in the time, Daniel had to bite back at the bile that persistently threatened to fill his mouth. He thought of his mother. Jesse. But selfishly, it always came back to him. What did they want from him? What were they going to do?

The drive was long enough for Daniel's raw skin to begin stinging, painfully throbbing and sending nerves screaming with every pothole the vehicle seemed to carelessly speed over. He imagined how he looked, sprawled in the footwell of some car, head censored by a rough, brown burlap sack, his arms helplessly bound behind his back by a digging zip tie, that, with every small shift, threatened to cut off his blood supply. If only somebody looked through the windows and saw him, surely then he would be saved. But a whisper of doubt told him that the windows were tinted, nobody would save him.

Daniel's mouth was pressed against the sack and seat, stopping him from opening it and communicating with his abductors, leaving him to instead resort to grunts and humming to probe the driver. In the first initial attempts to communicate, Daniel was met with stone cold silence, but after his persistent humming he finally got a response - "Thut up!", the speaker's lisp and venom audible through the sack, and Daniel obliged, partly for fear of getting hurt any further and also because he had found out what he wanted to know. The voice that had answered him had come from across him, rather than directly in front where the steering wheel was situated meaning that the driver had remained silent and that there was another passenger riding shotgun.

Daniel closed his eyes, who were these people? In an instant Alan had gotten at least five men to handle Daniel, receiving no friction with his removal in a relatively busy part of the day. Daniel mused that it was around two when things kicked off, meaning there should have been plenty of witnesses, however there was none, and looking back, it began to dawn upon Daniel just how sketchy the area surrounding Mega Emporium casino was. All those closed businesses and idle, loitering pedestrians with sticky eyes that Daniel brushed off as part of the casino effect.

The car stopped, a window rolled down, some indistinct chatter signalled the driver talking with someone outside and then the car rolled again, as if held at some sort of checkpoint. Moments later the car stopped again, this time the driver turned the engine off and exited the vehicle. Daniel teeth rattled as two door slams meant he was alone in the vehicle, a thought that he cherished for a second before two doors opened and he was hoisted up onto somebody's shoulder, changes in environment marked by different sounds of footsteps. It began with gravel, marble, carpet – coupled with grunts that told Daniel that they were climbing stairs, and finally wood. Once in the wooden floored room, Daniel felt fingers fiddling with his hands and suddenly they were free. Before Daniel could flex his sore, half-strangled wrists to encourage blood flow, he was deposited like a sack of potatoes into a chair, its padding doing little to absorb the jarring impact felt by Daniel.

The bag was torn off his head, blinding light rushing into his eyes, tearing at his face as if trying to cling on, narrowly failing to remove his false moustache. As Daniel vulnerably sat there, blinking frantically, the men who escorted him had stepped back somewhere behind Daniel, ready to act at a moment's notice in the case of misbehaviour. Eyes finally acclimatising to the light, Daniel's hungry eyes darted around the room, confirming that the floor was made of a rich, chocolate brown wood, its glossed planks void of any tree knots and other imperfections.

The walls were a pure white, given depth with swirling ledges and hidden LEDs. Finally turning his attention to what was in front of him, he sat across a marble table, marked with its default black scars, and an imposing black leather chair, its height boldened by the expansive book shelve behind it. The chair swivelled around, revealing a fireplace neatly incorporated into the wall, lined with additional marble and with flames roaring like a dog barking at an intruder. The man in the chair was Alan. He had changed from the black suit and tie he wore at the casino into a more comfortable dinner jacket, with a top-opened shirt beneath. The only thing that remained the same was his oily, black hair and the entrepreneurial, predatorial glint in his eyes. The move was so cliché that Daniel could not help but ask," Where's the cat?"

Alan paused, momentarily confused but caught on quickly, a wicked look catching Daniel off guard, "It's right here." He clicked his tongue and from behind his chair a white leopard arose from its position by the warm fire. Blue eyes piercing through Daniel as it padded closer, its progress recorded the metallic clinking of chains being undone, chains that kept the leopard restrained. Daniel had never seen a leopard outside a zoo, and its white body meant it was a snow leopard. He recalled that snow leopards were one of the most endangered animals on the planet, never expecting to be in the same room as one. The leopard padded back, curious eyes still fixated on the newcomer before yawning, exposing teeth as long as Daniel's fingers, and lying back down by the fire and out of Daniel's view.

Alan grinned, his first genuine smile since meeting Daniel as he drank in his fear. "Dan! Eyes up here, please." Alan had brought a small wooden, box to rest onto the table and extracted its content letting it catch the glint of the first behind him before tearing off his cruel eyes off the revolver's glossy cover and fixing them on Daniel, a manic smile threatening to spray across his face. "Daniel... you made me look like a fool today!" Alan laughed "You may have noticed that I have quite an influence in Mega Emporium, and that's because I am the director of the establishment"; no longer interested in Daniel, he snapped open the cylinder of the gun, revealing six empty chambers, and rummaged around in the box as he continued speaking. "You made me lose some money... but that's alright." Alan retrieved a single golden bullet from the box and slotted it into one of the chambers. "Money doesn't matter to me," Alan clicked the cylinder back into its place, closing his eyes as he savoured the snap that punctured the room. "Are you familiar with Russian roulette, Dan?" Alan turned his eyes back to Daniel, who nodded, having watched enough movies to know the basics. "Good." Alan spun the cylinder, filling the silence with a rapid clicking noise. "Time to see if you are really lucky, or just a filthy cheater" Alan gave a Daniel a look of superiority as he raised the barrel back into the air, letting it catch light. "What? I- I never cheate-" a raised finger silenced him; and Daniel decided it best to obey the person with the gun, "That's what we'll be finding out shortly. The chambers are already mixed."

Alan looked over Daniel's shoulder and motioned to the men behind him to leave and waited until a sturdy thud of the panelled door closing finalised their exit, before spinning the revolver across the table to Daniel. "If you try anything with the revolver that I don't like, I have a pistol that I'll use." Alan pulled his jacket sideways to reveal a more modern, aggressive looking pistol holstered on his chest, "You may proceed."

Daniel picked up the revolver with clammy hands, a slight tremor in his arm threatening to drop the gun. As Daniel brought the pistol's muzzle to his head, he closed his eyes, leaving himself momentarily alone in the darkness with the screaming voice of survival which resounded in his skull. Head throbbing against the cold metal barrel pressed against the side of his head.

Six chambers, one bullet, five shots, no choice. He opened them again, purging his mind of any hesitation, catching the faces of his mother, of Jesse -

even his dad as he emptied his brain of anything that would stop him from firing the gun. Approaching a state of hyperventilation, Daniel inwardly screamed a prayer before severing his body's will of self-preservation and pulled the trigger.

Acknowledgements

Firstly, you wouldn't be reading this if it wasn't for the Mark Evison Foundation and their noble aim to help students fulfil their aspirations in the form of a challenge. Writing 'Against the Odds' has been difficult, but very enjoyable, something I can tick off my bucket list and for that I must say a huge thank you to, more specifically, Margaret for sharing her own experience with book writing to help me with mine, and Frieda for helping me organise my application to have this challenge approved. Thank you to my dad for helping me format the book and for pushing me to write more than the previously established 250 words per day, a figure which turned to 500 and later, 1000. Thank you to my mother for her support and consolidation while I wrote my book. Thank you to my siblings, for agreeing to help me proof-read early copies of the book, allowing me to identify key, embarrassing mistakes that I'm glad didn't make it to the final product. I've also got to say thank you to Ahmad for helping come up with the idea for Daniel's power and designing the cover, Matt for giving me way too many ideas I couldn't include (nuclear fission in the next one, eh?) and Ragge for inadvertently helping me balance what seemed like an overpowered ability.

Charity Edition

Only 50 copies printed.